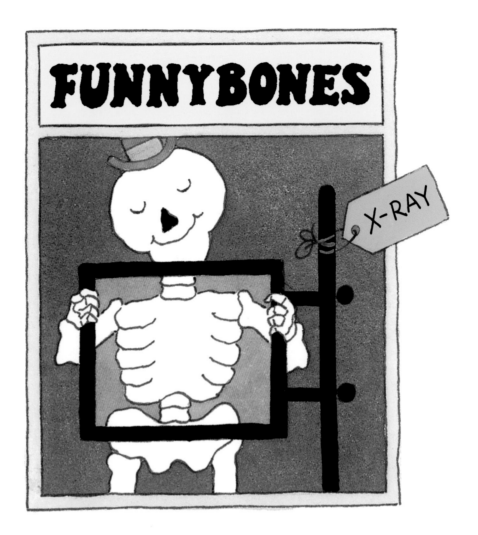

Bumps in the Night

ALLAN AHLBERG • ANDRÉ AMSTUTZ

PUFFIN

In the dark dark cellar
of a dark dark house,
a little skeleton is reading a comic.
In the dark dark street
of a dark dark town,
a big skeleton is walking the dog.

Then the big one hurries home,
and the little one hurries out,
and – "Help!" –
they go bump in the night.

In the dark dark classroom
of a dark dark Night School,
a little skeleton is painting a picture.
In the dark dark workshop
of the same Night School,
a big skeleton is making a chair.

Then the little one takes his picture
to show the big one,
and the big one takes his chair
to show the little one,
and – "Wow!" –
they go bump in the night again.

"Send for Doctor Bones!"

The little skeleton and the big skeleton
walk *carefully* to the park.
They swing on the swings,
throw a stick for the dog
and play football.

The leg bone's connected to the foot bone,"
the little one sings.
The foot bone's connected to the ball."

"The head bone's connected
to the – (CLONK!) – head bone,"
cries the big one.

"Send for Doctor Bones!"

The little skeleton and
the big skeleton sit
– but not too close together –
in the dark dark cellar.
"This is a dark dark cellar,"
says the little one. "Let's paint it."
"Good idea!" the big one says.

The big skeleton
and the little skeleton
paint the cellar
and, now and then, the dog.

They paint the cellar
red and green and blue,
and lots more colours.

But . . .
"It's still dark,"
the little skeleton says.
"Let's paint it white."
So, they paint it white . . .

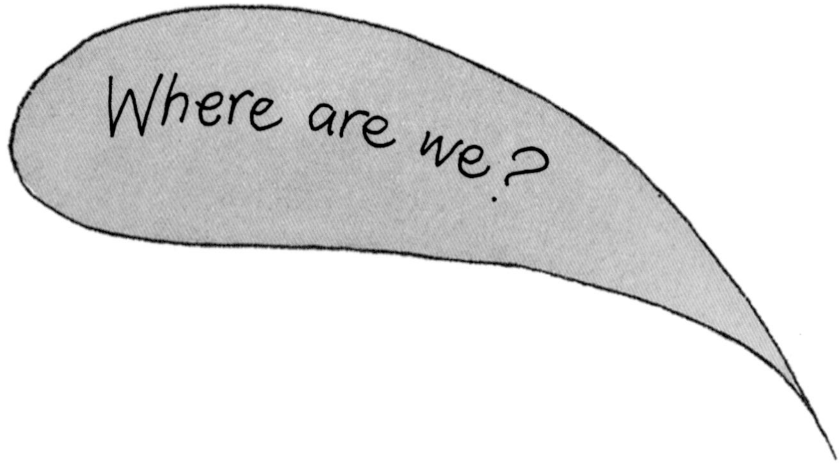
Where are we?

and disappear!
And – you guessed it –
go bump in the night.

"Send for Doctor Bones!"

After that . . .
they go bump in the night playing tennis
and bump in the night playing golf.

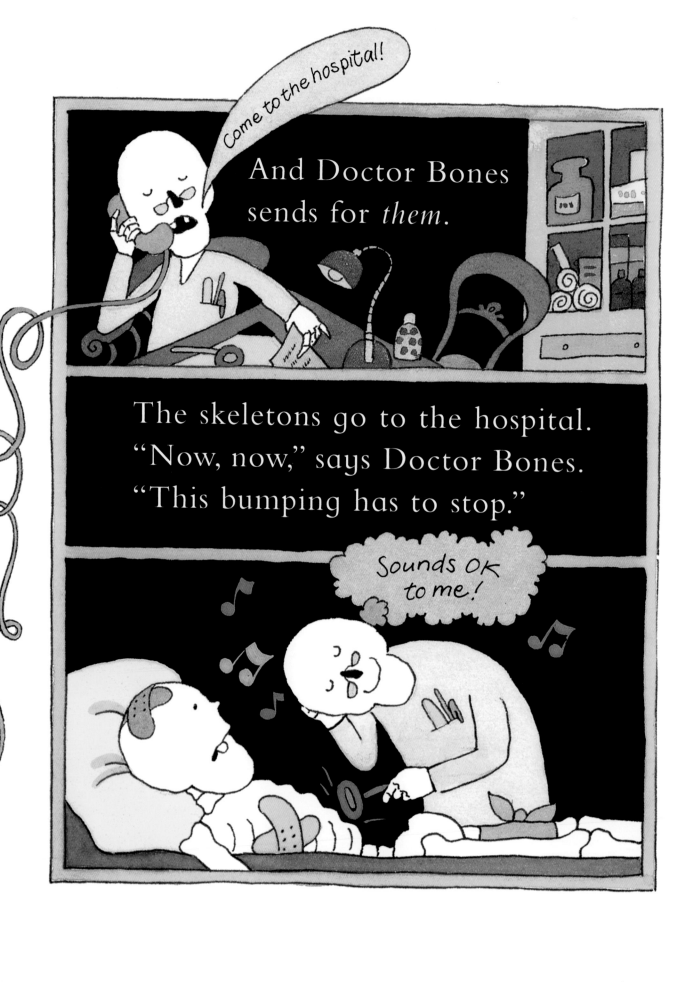

In the dark dark cellar
(they painted it black again)
of a dark dark house,
a little skeleton is fast asleep.
"Zzz!"

In the same cellar of the same house,
a big skeleton is fast asleep too.
"Zzz!"

There they are . . .
tucked up snug and safe at last
from bumps in the night.

Well, nearly.

The End

PUFFIN BOOKS

UK | USA | Canada | Ireland | Australia
India | New Zealand | South Africa

Puffin Books is part of the Penguin Random House group of companies
whose addresses can be found at global.penguinrandomhouse.com.

www.penguin.co.uk   www.puffin.co.uk   www.ladybird.co.uk

 Penguin
Random House
UK

First published by William Heinemann Ltd 1993
First published in Puffin Books 2005
This edition published 2018

001

Printed in China
A CIP catalogue record for this book is available from the British Library

ISBN: 978–0–241–37764–2

All correspondence to:
Puffin Books, Penguin Random House Children's
80 Strand, London WC2R 0RL

MIX
Paper from
responsible sources
FSC® C018179